THE MATCH

BY

JAMES OLIVER CURWOOD

British Library Cataloguing-in-Publication Data
A catalogue record for this book is available from the
British Library

James Oliver Curwood

James Oliver 'Jim' Curwood was an American action-adventure writer and conservationist. He was born on 12th June, 1878, in Owosso, Michigan, USA – as the youngest of four children.

He left high school before graduation, but passed the entrance exam to the University of Michigan, where he enrolled in the English department and studied journalism. After two years, he quit college to become a reporter. In 1900, Curwood sold his first story while working for the Detroit News-Tribune, and after this, his career in writing was made. By 1909 he had saved enough money to travel to the Canadian northwest, a trip that provided the inspiration for his wilderness adventure stories. The success of his novels afforded him the opportunity to return to the Yukon and Alaska for several months each year – allowing Curwood to write more than thirty such books.

By 1922, Curwood's writings had made him a very wealthy man and he fulfilled a childhood fantasy by building 'Curwood Castle' in Owosso. Constructed in the style of an eighteenth century French Chateau, the estate overlooked the Shiawassee River, and made for a truly picturesque setting. In one of the homes' two large turrets, Curwood set up his writing studio. He also owned a camp in a remote area in Baraga County, Michigan, near the Huron Mountains as well as a cabin in Roscommon, Michigan.

Curwood's adventure writing followed in the tradition of Jack London. Like London, Curwood set many of his works in the wilds of the Great Northwest and often used animals as lead characters (Kazan, Baree; Son of Kazan, The Grizzly King and Nomads of the North). Many of Curwood's adventure novels also feature romance as primary or secondary plot consideration. This approach gave his work broad commercial appeal and helped drive his appearance on several best-seller lists in the early 1920s. His most successful work was his 1920 novel, The River's End. The book sold more than 100,000 copies and was the fourth best-selling title of the year in the United States, according to Publisher's Weekly. He contributed to various literary and popular magazines throughout his career, and his bibliography includes more than 200 such articles, short stories and serializations.

Curwood was an avid hunter in his youth; however, as he grew older, he became an advocate of environmentalism and was appointed to the 'Michigan Conservation Commission' in 1926. The change in his attitude toward wildlife can be best expressed by a quote he gave in The Grizzly King: that 'The greatest thrill is not to kill but to let live.' Despite this change in attitude, Curwood did not have an ultimately fruitful relationship with nature. In 1927, while on a fishing trip in Florida, Curwood was bitten on the thigh by what was believed to have been a spider and he had an immediate allergic reaction. Health problems related to the bite escalated over the next few months as an infection set in. He died soon after in his nearby home on Williams Street, on 13th August 1927. He was aged just forty-nine, and was interred in Oak Hill Cemetery (Owosso), in a family plot.

Curwood's legacy lives on however, and his home of Curwood Castle is now a museum. During the first full weekend in June of each year, the city of Owosso holds the Curwood Festival to celebrate the city's heritage, and in addition, a mountain in L'Anse Township, Michigan was given the name Mount Curwood, and the L'Anse Township Park was renamed Curwood Park.

THE MATCH

Sergeant Brokaw was hatchet-faced, with shifting pale blue eyes that had a glint of cruelty in them. He was tall, and thin, and lithe as a cat. He belonged to the Royal Northwest Mounted Police, and was one of the best men on the trail that had ever gone into the North. His business was man hunting. Ten years of seeking after human prey had given to him many of the characteristics of a fox. For six of those ten years he had represented law north of fifty-three. Now he had come to the end of his last hunt, close up to the Arctic Circle. For one hundred and eighty-seven days he had been following a man. The hunt had begun in midsummer, and it was now midwinter. Billy Loring, who was wanted for murder, had been a hard man to find. But he was caught at last, and Brokaw was keenly exultant. It was his greatest achievement. It would mean a great deal for him down at headquarters.

In the rough and dimly lighted cabin his man sat opposite him, on a bench, his manacled hands crossed over his knees. He was a younger man than Brokaw—thirty, or a little better. His hair was long, reddish, and untrimmed. A stubble of reddish beard covered his face. His eyes, too, were blue—of the deep, honest blue that one remembers, and most frequently trusts. He did not look like a criminal. There was something almost boyish in his face, a little hollowed by long privation. He was the sort of man that other men liked. Even Brokaw, who had a heart like flint in the face of crime, had melted a little.

"Ugh!" he shivered. "Listen to that beastly wind! It means three days of storm." Outside a gale was blowing straight down from the Arctic. They could hear the steady moaning of it in the spruce tops over the cabin, and now and then there came one of those raging blasts that filled the night with strange shrieking sounds. Volleys of fine, hard snow beat against the one window with a rattle like shot. In the cabin it was comfortable. It was Billy's cabin. He had built it deep in a swamp, where there were lynx and fisher cat to trap, and where he had thought that no one could find him. The sheet-iron stove was glowing hot. An oil lamp hung from the ceiling. Billy was sitting so that the glow of this fell in his face. It scintillated on the rings of steel about his wrists. Brokaw was a cautious man, as well as a clever one, and he took no chances.

"I like storms—when you're inside, an' close to a stove," replied Billy. "Makes me feel sort of—safe." He smiled a little grimly. Even at that it was not an unpleasant smile.

Brokaw's snow-reddened eyes gazed at the other.

"There's something in that," he said. "This storm will give you at least three days more of life."

"Won't you drop that?" asked the prisoner, turning his face a little, so that it was shaded from the light.

"You've got me now, an' I know what's coming as well as you do." His voice was low and quiet, with the faintest trace of a broken note in it, deep down in his throat. "We're alone, old man, and a long way from anyone. I ain't blaming you for catching me. I haven't got anything against you. So let's drop this other thing—what I'm going down to—and talk something pleasant. I know I'm going to hang. That's the law. It'll be pleasant enough when it comes, don't you think? Let's talk about—about—home. Got any kids?"

Brokaw shook his head, and took his pipe from his mouth.

"Never married," he said shortly.

"Never married," mused Billy, regarding him with a curious softening of his blue eyes. "You don't know what you've missed, Brokaw. Of course, it's none of my business, but you've got a home—somewhere—" Brokaw shook his head again.

"Been in the service ten years," he said. "I've got a mother living with my brother somewhere down in York State. I've sort of lost track of them. Haven't seen 'em in five years."

Billy was looking at him steadily. Slowly he rose to his feet, lifted his manacled hands, and turned down the light.

"Hurts my eyes," he said, and he laughed frankly as he caught the suspicious glint in Brokaw's eyes. He seated himself again, and leaned over toward the other. "I haven't talked to a white man for three months," he added, a little hesitatingly. "I've been hiding—close. I had a dog for a time, and he died, an' I didn't dare go hunting for another. I knew you fellows were pretty close after me. But I wanted to get enough fur to take me to South America. Had it all planned, an' SHE was going to join me there—with the kid. Understand? If you'd kept away another month—"

There was a husky break in his voice, and he coughed to clear it.

"You don't mind if I talk, do you—about her, an' the kid? I've got to do it, or bust, or go mad. I've got to because—to-day—she was twenty-four—at ten o'clock in the morning—an' it's our wedding day—"

The half gloom hid from Brokaw what was in the other's face. And then Billy laughed almost joyously. "Say, but she's been a true little pardner," he whispered proudly, as there came a lull in the storm. "She was just born for me, an' everything seemed to happen on her birthday, an' that's why I can't be downhearted even NOW. It's her birthday? you see, an' this morning, before you came, I was just that happy that I set a plate for her at the table, an' put her picture and a curl of her hair beside it—set the picture up so it was looking at me—an' we had breakfast together. Look here—"

8

He moved to the table, with Brokaw watching him like a cat, and brought something back with him, wrapped in a soft piece of buckskin. He unfolded the buckskin tenderly, and drew forth a long curl that rippled a dull red and gold in the lamp-glow, and then he handed a photograph to Brokaw.

"That's her!" he whispered.

Brokaw turned so that the light fell on the picture. A sweet, girlish face smiled at him from out of a wealth of flowing, disheveled curls.

"She had it taken that way just for me," explained Billy, with the enthusiasm of a boy in his voice. "She's always wore her hair in curls—an' a braid—for me, when we're home. I love it that way. Guess I may be silly but I'll tell you why. THAT was down in York State, too. She lived in a cottage, all grown over with honeysuckle an' morning glory, with green hills and valleys all about it—and the old apple orchard just behind. That day we were in the orchard all red an' white with bloom, and she dared me to a race. I let her beat me, and when I came up she stood under one of the trees, her cheeks like the pink blossoms, and her hair all tumbled about her like an armful of gold, shaking the loose apple blossoms down on her head. I forgot everything then, and I didn't stop until I had her in my arms, an'—an' she's been my little pardner ever since. After the baby came we moved up into Canada, where I had a good chance in a new mining town. An' then—" A furious blast of the storm sent the overhanging spruce tops smashing against the top of the cabin. Straight overhead the wind shrieked almost like human voices, and the one window rattled as though it were shaken by human hands. The lamp had been burning lower and lower. It began to flicker now, the quick sputter of the wick lost in the noise of the gale. Then it went out. Brokaw leaned over and opened the door of the big box stove, and the red glow of the fire took the place of the lamplight. He leaned back and relighted his pipe, eyeing Billy. The sudden blast, the going out of the light, the opening of the stove door, had all happened in a minute, but the interval was long enough to bring a change in Billy's voice. It was cold and hard when he continued. He leaned over toward Brokaw, and the boyishness had gone from his face.

"Of course, I can't expect you to have any sympathy for this other business, Brokaw," he went on. "Sympathy isn't in your line, an' you wouldn't be the big man you are in the service if you had it. But I'd like to know what YOU would have done. We were up there six months, and we'd both grown to love the big woods, and she was growing prettier and happier every day—when Thorne, the new superintendent, came up. One day she told me that she didn't like Thorne, but I didn't pay much attention to that, and laughed at her, and said he was a good fellow. After that I could see that something was worrying her, and pretty soon I couldn't help from seeing what it was, and everything came out. It was Thorne. He was persecuting her. She hadn't told me, because she knew it would make trouble and I'd lose my job. One afternoon I came home earlier than usual, and found her crying. She put her arms round my neck, and just cried it all out, with her face snuggled in my neck, and kissin' me—"

Brokaw could see the cords in Billy's neck. His manacled hands were clenched.

"What would you have done, Brokaw?" he asked huskily. "What if you had a wife, an' she told you that another man had insulted her, and was forcing his attentions on her, and she asked you to give up your job and take her away? Would you have done it, Brokaw? No, you wouldn't. You'd have hunted up the man. That's what I did. He had been drinking—just enough to make him devilish, and he laughed at me—I didn't mean to strike so hard.—But it happened. I killed him. I got away. She and the baby are down in the little cottage again—down in York State—an' I know she's awake this minute—our wedding day—thinking of me, an' praying for me, and counting the days between now and spring. We were going to South America then."

Brokaw rose to his feet, and put fresh wood into the stove.

"I guess it must be pretty hard," he said, straightening himself. "But the law up here doesn't take them things into account—not very much. It may let you off with

11

manslaugher—ten or fifteen years. I hope it does. Let's turn in."

Billy stood up beside him. He went with Brokaw to a bunk built against the wall, and the sergeant drew a fine steel chain from his pocket. Billy lay down, his hands crossed over his breast, and Brokaw deftly fastened the chain about his ankles.

"And I suppose you think THIS is hard, too," he added. "But I guess you'd do it if you were me. Ten years of this sort of work learns you not to take chances. If you want anything in the night just whistle." It had been a hard day with Brokaw, and he slept soundly. For an hour Billy lay awake, thinking of home, and listening to the wail of the storm. Then he, too, fell into sleep—a restless, uneasy slumber filled with troubled visions. For a time there had come a lull in the storm, but now it broke over the cabin with increased fury. A hand seemed slapping at the window, threatening to break it. The spruce boughs moaned and twisted overhead, and a volley of wind and snow shot suddenly down the chimney, forcing open the stove door, so that a shaft of ruddy light cut like a red knife through the dense gloom of the cabin. In varying ways the sounds played a part in Billy's dreams. In all those dreams, and segments of dreams, the girl—his wife—was present. Once they had gone for wild flowers and had been caught in a thunderstorm, and had run to an old and disused barn in the middle of a field for shelter.

12

He was back in that barn again, with HER—and he could feel her trembling against him, and he was stroking her hair, as the thunder crashed over them and the lightning filled her eyes with fear. After that there came to him a vision of the early autumn nights when they had gone corn roasting, with other young people. He had always been afflicted with a slight nasal trouble, and smoke irritated him. It set him sneezing, and kept him dodging about the fire, and she had always laughed when the smoke persisted in following him about, like a young scamp of a boy bent on tormenting him. The smoke was unusually persistent to-night. He tossed in his bunk, and buried his face in the blanket that answered for a pillow. The smoke reached him even there, and he sneezed chokingly. In that instant the girl's face disappeared. He sneezed again—and awoke.

A startled gasp broke from his lips, and the handcuffs about his wrists clanked as he raised his hands to his face. In that moment his dazed senses adjusted themselves. The cabin was full of smoke. It partly blinded him, but through it he could see tongues of fire shooting toward the ceiling. He could hear the crackling of burning pitch, and he yelled wildly to Brokaw. In an instant the sergeant was on his feet. He rushed to the table, where he had placed a pail of water the evening before, and Billy heard the hissing of the water as it struck the flaming wall.

"Never mind that," he shouted. "The shack's built of pitch cedar. We've got to get out!" Brokaw groped his way to him through the smoke and began fumbling at the chain about his ankles.

"I can't—find—the key—" he gasped chokingly. "Here grab hold of me!"

He caught Billy under the arms and dragged him to the door. As he opened it the wind came in with a rush and behind them the whole cabin burst into a furnace of flame. Twenty yards from the cabin he dropped Billy in the snow, and ran back. In that seething room of smoke and fire was everything on which their lives depended, food, blankets, even their coats and caps and snowshoes. But he could go no farther than the door. He returned to Billy, found the key in his pocket, and freed him from the chain about his ankles. Billy stood up. As he looked at Brokaw the glass in the window broke and a sea of flame sprouted through. It lighted up their faces. The sergeant's jaw was set hard. His leathery face was curiously white. He could not keep from shivering. There was a strange smile on Billy's face, and a strange look in his eyes. Neither of the two men had undressed for sleep, but their coats, and caps, and heavy mittens were in the flames.

Billy rattled his handcuffs. Brokaw looked him squarely in the eyes.

"You ought to know this country," he said. "What'll we do?"

"The nearest post is sixty miles from here," said Billy.

"I know that," replied Brokaw. "And I know that Thoreau's cabin is only twenty miles from here. There must be some trapper or Indian shack nearer than that. Is there?" In the red glare of the fire Billy smiled. His teeth gleamed at Brokaw. It was a lull of the wind, and he went close to Brokaw, and spoke quietly, his eyes shining more and more with that strange light that had come into them.

"This is going to be a big sight easier than hanging, or going to jail for half my life, Brokaw—an' you don't think I'm going to be fool enough to miss the chance, do you? It ain't hard to die of cold. I've almost been there once or twice. I told you last night why I couldn't give up hope— that something good for me always came on her birthday, or near to it. An' it's come. It's forty below, an' we won't live the day out. We ain't got a mouthful of grub. We ain't got clothes enough on to keep us from freezing inside the shanty, unless we had a fire. Last night I saw you fill your match bottle and put it in your coat pocket. Why, man, WE AIN'T EVEN GOT A MATCH!"

In his voice there was a thrill of triumph. Brokaw's hands were clenched, as if some one had threatened to strike him.

"You mean—" he gasped.

"Just this," interrupted Billy, and his voice was harder than Brokaw's now. "The God you used to pray to when you was a kid has given me a choice, Brokaw, an' I'm going to take it. If we stay by this fire, an' keep it up, we won't die of cold, but of starvation. We'll be dead before we get half way to Thoreau's. There's an Indian shack that we could make, but you'll never find it—not unless you unlock these irons and give me that revolver at your belt. Then I'll take you over there as my prisoner. That'll give me another chance for South America—an' the kid an' home." Brokaw was buttoning the thick collar of his shirt close up about his neck. On his face, too, there came for a moment a grim and determined smile.

"Come on," he said, "we'll make Thoreau's or die."

"Sure," said Billy, stepping quickly to his side. "I suppose I might lie down in the snow, an' refuse to budge. I'd win my game then, wouldn't I? But we'll play it—on the square. It's Thoreau's, or die. And it's up to you to find Thoreau's."

He looked back over his shoulder at the burning cabin as they entered the edge of the forest, and in the gray darkness that was preceding dawn he smiled to himself. Two miles to the south, in a thick swamp, was Indian Joe's cabin. They could have made it easily. On their way to Thoreau's they would pass within a mile of it. But Brokaw would never know. And they would never reach Thoreau's. Billy knew that. He looked at the man hunter as he broke trail ahead of him—at the pugnacious hunch of his shoulders, his long stride, the determined clench of his hands, and wondered what the soul and the heart of a man like this must be, who in such an hour would not trade life for life. For almost three-quarters of an hour Brokaw did not utter a word. The storm had broke. Above the spruce tops the sky began to clear. Day came slowly. And it was growing steadily colder. The swing of Brokaw'a arms and shoulders kept the blood in them circulating, while Billy's manacled wrists held a part of his body almost rigid. He knew that his hands were already frozen. His arms were numb, and when at last Brokaw paused for a moment on the edge of a frozen stream Billy thrust out his hands, and clanked the steel rings.

"It must be getting colder," he said. "Look at that."

The cold steel had seared his wrists like hot iron, and had pulled off patches of skin and flesh. Brokaw looked, and hunched his shoulders. His lips were blue. His cheeks, ears, and nose were frost-bitten. There was a curious thickness in his voice when he spoke.

"Thoreau lives on this creek," he said. "How much farther is it?"

"Fifteen or sixteen miles," replied Billy. "You'll last just about five, Brokaw. I won't last that long unless you take these things off and give me the use of my arms."

"To knock out my brains when I ain't looking," growled Brokaw. "I guess—before long—you'll be willing to tell

17

where the Indian's shack is." He kicked his way through a drift of snow to the smoother surface of the stream. There was a breath of wind in their faces, and Billy bowed his head to it. In the hours of his greatest loneliness and despair Billy had kept up his fighting spirit by thinking of pleasant things, and now, as he followed in Brokaw's trail, he began to think of home. It was not hard for him to bring up visions of the girl wife who would probably never know how he had died. He forgot Brokaw. He followed in the trail mechanically, failing to notice that his captor's pace was growing steadily slower, and that his own feet were dragging more and more like leaden weights. He was back among the old hills again, and the sun was shining, and he heard laughter and song. He saw Jeanne standing at the gate in front of the little white cottage, smiling at him, and waving Baby Jeanne's tiny hand at him as he looked back over his shoulder from down the dusty road. His mind did not often travel as far as the mining camp, and he had completely forgotten it now. He no longer felt the sting and pain of the intense cold. It was Brokaw who brought him back into the reality of things. The sergeant stumbled and fell in a drift, and Billy fell over him. For a moment the two men sat half buried in the snow, looking at each other without speaking. Brokaw moved first. He rose to his feet with an effort. Billy made an attempt to follow him. After three efforts he gave it up, and blinked up into Brokaw's face with a queer laugh. The laugh was almost soundless. There had come a change in Brokaw's face. Its determination and confidence were gone. At last the iron mask of the Law was broken, and there shone through it something of the emotions and the brotherhood of man. He was fumbling in one of his pockets, and drew out the key to the handcuffs. It was a small key, and he held it between his stiffened fingers with diffic ulty. He knelt down beside Billy. The keyhole was filled with snow. It took a long time—ten minutes—before the key was fitted in and the lock clicked. He helped to tear off the cuffs. Billy felt no sensation as bits of skin and flesh came "with them. Brokaw gave him a hand, and assisted him to rise. For the first time he spoke.

"Guess you've got me beat, Billy," he said.

"Where's the Indian's?"

He drew his revolver from its holster and tossed it in the snowdrift. The shadow of a smile passed grimly over his face. Billy looked about him. They had stopped where the frozen path of a smaller stream joined the creek. He raised one of his stiffened arms and pointed to it.

"Follow that creek—four miles—and you'll come to Indian Joe's shack," he said.

"And a mile is just about our limit"

"Just about—your's," replied Billy. "I can't make another half. If we had a fire—"

"IF—" wheezed Brokaw.

"If we had a fire," continued Billy. "We could warm ourselves, an' make the Indian's shack easy, couldn't we?"

Brokaw did not answer. He had turned toward the creek when one of Billy's pulseless hands fell heavily on his arm.

"Look here, Brokaw."

Brokaw turned. They looked into each other's eyes.

"I guess mebby you're a man, Brokaw," said Billy quietly. "You've done what you thought was your duty. You've kept your word to th' law, an' I believe you'll keep your word with me. If I say the word that'll save us now will you go back to headquarters an' report me dead?" For a full half minute their eyes did not waver.

Then Brokaw said:

"No."

Billy dropped his hand. It was Brokaw's hand that fell on his arm now.

"I can't do that," he said. "In ten years I ain't run out the white flag once. It's something that ain't known in the service. There ain't a coward in it, or a man who's afraid to die. But I'll play you square. I'll wait until we're both on our feet, again, and then I'll give you twenty-four hours the start of me."

Billy was smiling now. His hand reached out. Brokaw's met it, and the two joined in a grip that their numb fingers scarcely felt.

"Do you know," said Billy softly, "there's been somethin' runnin' in my head ever since we left the burning cabin. It's something my mother taught me: 'Do unto others as you'd have others do unto you.' I'm a d—- fool, ain't I? But I'm goin' to try the experiment, Brokaw, an' see what comes of it. I could drop in a snowdrift an' let you go on—to die. Then I could save myself. But I'm going to take your word—an' do the other thing. I'VE GOT A MATCH."

"A MATCH!"

"Just one. I remember dropping it in my pants pocket yesterday when I was out on the trail. It's in THIS pocket. Your hand is in better shape than mine. Get it."

Life had leaped into Brokaw's face. He thrust his hand into Billy's pocket, staring at him as he fumbled, as if fearing that he had lied. When he drew his hand out the match was between his fingers.

"Ah!" he whispered excitedly.

"Don't get nervous," warned Billy. "It's the only one."

Brokaw's eyes were searching the low timber along the shore. "There's a birch tree," he cried. "Hold it—while I gather a pile of bark!"

He gave the match to Billy, and staggered through the snow to the bank. Strip after strip of the loose bark he tore from the tree. Then he gathered it in a heap in the shelter of a low-hanging spruce, and added dry sticks, and still more bark, to it. When it was ready he stood with his hands in his pockets, and looked at Billy.

"If we had a stone, an' a piece of paper—" he began.

Billy thrust a hand that felt like lifeless lead inside his shirt, and fumbled in a pocket he had made there. Brokaw watched him with red, eager eyes. The hand reappeared, and in it was the buckskin wrapped photograph he had seen the night before, Billy took off the buckskin. About the picture there was a bit of tissue paper. He gave this and the match to Brokaw.

"There's a little gun-file in the pocket the match came from," he said. "I had it mending a trapchain. You can scratch the match on that."

He turned so that Brokaw could reach into the pocket, and the man hunter thrust in his hand. When he brought it forth he held the file. There was a smile on Billy's frostbitten face as he held the picture for a moment under Brokaw's eyes. Billy's own hands had ruffled up the girl's shining curls an instant before the picture was taken, and she was laughing at him when the camera clicked.

"It's all up to her, Brokaw," Billy said gently. "I told you that last night. It was she who woke me up before the fire got us. If you ever prayed—pray a little now. FOR SHE'S GOING TO STRIKE THAT MATCH!"

He still looked at the picture as Brokaw knelt beside the pile he had made. He heard the scratch of the match on the file, but his eyes did not turn. The living, breathing face of the most beautiful thing in the world was speaking to him from out of that picture. His mind was dazed. He swayed a little. He heard a voice, low and sweet, and so distant that it came to him like the faintest whisper. "I am coming—I am coming, Billy—coming—coming—coming—" A joyous cry surged up from his soul, but it died on his lips in a strange gasp. A louder cry brought him back to himself for a moment. It was from Brokaw. The sergeant's face was terrible to behold. He rose to his feet, swaying, his hands clutched at his breast. His voice was thick—hopeless.

"The match—went—out—" He staggered up to Billy, his eyes like a madman's. Billy swayed dizzily. He laughed, even as he crumpled down in the snow. As if in a dream he saw Brokaw stagger off on the frozen trail. He saw him disappear in his hopeless effort to reach the Indian's shack. And then a strange darkness closed him in, and in that darkness he heard still the sweet voice of his wife. It spoke his name again and again, and it urged him to wake up— wake up—WAKE UP! It seemed a long time before he could respond to it. But at last he opened his eyes. He dragged himself to his knees, and looked first to find Brokaw. But the man hunter had gone—forever. The picture was still in his hand. Less distinctly than before he saw the girl smiling at him. And then—at his back—he heard a strange and new sound. With an effort he turned to discover what it was.

The match had hidden an unseen spark from Brokaw's eyes. From out of the pile of fuel was rising a pillar of smoke and flame.

.

www.ingramcontent.com/pod-product-compliance
Lightning Source LLC
Chambersburg PA
CBHW030137260626
47156CB00008B/2976

* 9 7 8 1 4 7 3 3 2 5 8 2 1 *